I Love You Fur-ever

Alondra

Suzanne Marshall

LiveWellMedia.com

ISBN: 9781090124531

This book is dedicated to
the paws-itively awesome

Alondra

ALONDRA,

let's help some
doggies settle down.
So no more barks
or racing around
or digging, jumping,
acting like clowns.
It's time for cozy
bedtime now.

You will always be my sunshine

You Are
Loved

Biscuits

As one dog
gets ready
to snooze,
remember

ALONDRA

I love you.

As two doggies
rest their paws,
I love you

ALONDRA

just because.

As three doggies
lay down their tails,
I love you

ALONDRA

without fail.

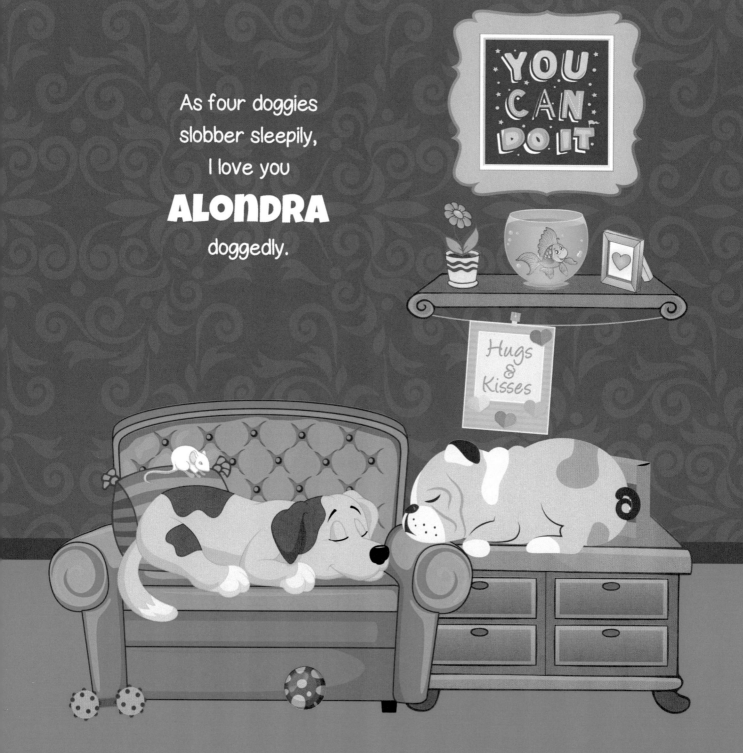

As four doggies
slobber sleepily,
I love you

ALONDRA

doggedly.

As five doggies
roll over
and doze,
I love you

ALONDRA

from your head
to your toes.

As six doggies
curl up and rest,
I love you

ALONDRA

with tail-wagging zest!

Love
is
the
answer

You are
always
in my
heart

ALONDRA,
as seven doggies
fall asleep,
I love you more
than puppies pee,
and that's a lot,
believe you me!

BE YOU

You are beautiful

As eight doggies
snort and snore,
I love you

ALONDRA

forevermore.

As nine doggies dream
of chasing squirrels,
I love you

ALONDRA

to the ends
of the world.

As the tenth doggy
hits the sack,
I love you

ALONDRA

to the moon
and back.

All ten doggies sleep at last,
plus one little kitty cat.
Now

ALONDRA

you can relax.

As you nestle down to sleep,
remember: I love you
a doggone heap!

♡✕♡✕

Alondra

More Personalized Books from LiveWellMedia.com

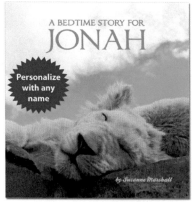

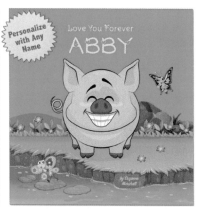

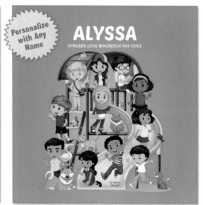

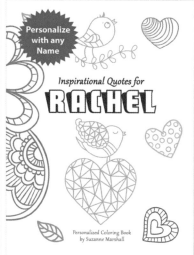

Credits

Big thanks to Mom and Dad, Don Marshall, Nathaniel Robinson, and Hannah and Rachel Roeder. All illustrations have been edited by the author. Original vectors by fotosearch artists: © Tigatelu, Dazdraperma, Hermandesign2015, Platinka, Anuchitas1917, ClaireV, Colematt, Frenta. Additional vectors curated from freepik.

About the Author

An honors graduate of Smith College, Suzanne Marshall writes to inspire, engage and empower children. Learn more about Suzanne and her books at **LiveWellMedia.com**.

(Photo: Suzanne Marshall & Abby Underdog)

Made in the USA
Las Vegas, NV
02 May 2022